GOODNIGHT AOI

THE DREAM OF US, FOREVER

PRATIK MISHRA

Made with ♥ on the Notion Press Platform
www.notionpress.com

To Aoi,
For teaching me that dreams are more than fleeting whispers,
And that love, in all its forms, transcends time and space.
This story is for you — forever a part of my soul.

And to those who still believe in the magic of stars, rivers, and the
quiet whispers of the heart — may you always find the courage to
chase the dreams that call to you.

Contents

Foreword

Stories have the power to transport us — to places we have never been, to emotions we have never fully understood, and to connections that feel both impossible and inevitable.
This book was born from a single thought: What if two souls, separated by worlds, were always meant to find each other?

In these pages, you will walk alongside Haruki and witness a journey woven with dreams, memories, and an unexplainable pull of destiny.
It is not just a tale of love; it is a tribute to hope, resilience, and the unseen threads that bind us to something greater than ourselves.

As you turn each page, I invite you to let go — of logic, of doubt — and simply feel.
Let the story whisper to the quiet corners of your heart.

Thank you for trusting me with your time, your imagination, and your emotions.
Welcome to a world where dreams breathe, rivers speak, and love never truly fades.

— Pratik Mishra

Preface

Every story begins with a feeling — a fleeting emotion, a forgotten dream, a silent "what if."
This story began with a simple image in my mind: a boy standing by a river, feeling an invisible presence pulling at his heart.

I have always been fascinated by the idea that some connections in life are beyond explanation.
That sometimes, even without a face or a voice, someone can feel familiar — like a memory you never lived, yet deeply remember.

Through the journey of Aoi, I tried to explore the invisible threads that tie two souls across distances, dreams, and even lifetimes.

This is not just a love story — it is a story about faith: faith in feelings we can't name, in journeys we don't fully understand, and in endings that are really new beginnings.

Writing this book has been a deeply personal journey.
I hope that, in some small way, it finds a place in your heart, reminds you of your own silent hopes, and makes you believe — even for a moment — that unseen magic still exists in this world.

Thank you for being a part of this journey.

Acknowledgements

The journey of writing this book has been a beautiful blend of imagination, perseverance, and the support of many wonderful people.

I would like to express my heartfelt gratitude to my family and friends, who have stood by me through every high and low. Your unwavering encouragement gave me the strength to continue, even on the toughest days.

A special thanks to all the storytellers, dreamers, and readers who have inspired me through their words and passion. Your influence helped shape my own storytelling path.

I am also grateful for every quiet moment, every spark of inspiration, and every challenge along the way — all of which contributed to the making of this story.

Lastly, to my readers — thank you for choosing to embark on this journey. Your belief in stories and in the magic they hold gives writers like me a reason to keep creating.

This book is dedicated to all of you.

Prologue

In a world that often masks truth with illusion, some secrets refuse to stay buried.

Beneath the surface of everyday life, hidden stories whisper through forgotten streets and silent corners, waiting for someone to listen — or someone to awaken them.

This is not a story of heroes and villains, but of choices made in shadows, of silent battles fought within hearts, and of a destiny that quietly weaves itself through the lives of unsuspecting souls.

As the first page turns, so too begins a journey into the unknown — where reality blurs, and nothing is ever quite what it seems.

Are you ready to uncover what lies beyond the silence?

CHAPTER I

The Night We Met

The clock in Haruki Sato's apartment blinked 3:03 a.m., casting a pale green glow over the peeling walls.

Outside, Tokyo buzzed faintly, taxis sighing down empty streets, neon signs flickering against windows.

Inside, silence pressed heavy against Haruki's chest.

He sighed and turned in bed, staring at the cracked ceiling. Sleep was an old friend he had lost

somewhere along the way.

And yet tonight, sleep found him.

It began softly, a feeling of weightlessness, like drifting under water. When Haruki opened his eyes, he

was standing at the edge of a river that shimmered under a velvet sky.

The stars above spun slow dances. The river whispered to him.

And she was there.

A girl with black hair flowing like ink down her back, her skin pale under the silver light. She wore a simple

white dress, and when she smiled, Haruki felt the ground slip from beneath his feet.

"My name is Aoi," she said, laughter glimmering in her eyes.

Haruki didn't speak, he couldn't. But she took his hand gently, and in that touch, he found every word he

couldn't say.

They wandered the riverbanks, laughing, racing the wind. They spoke of forgotten places and childhood

dreams of stars they could never name.

Haruki woke with a start, his heart racing.

He rubbed his eyes, the warmth of her hand lingering against his fingers.

"A dream," he whispered into the empty room.

But the next night, she was waiting for him again.

This time, they built paper boats and sent them floating down the river, writing secret wishes on their

sails. They sang songs neither knew, yet both remembered. Under the stars, Haruki stole glances at her,

memorizing the curve of her smile, the tilt of her head when she laughed.

He had never known this kind of peace — this sense that the universe had bent its rules just for them.

Night after night, they met.

On the third night, Aoi led him to a field of sunflowers taller than either of them. They danced under the

open sky, spinning until they fall breathless onto the soft earth.Lying side by side, Aoi spoke of her home a small village near an old shrine called Toshimura. She

described mountains cradling the town, and the smell of summer rain on stone streets. Her voice was a

melody Haruki wished he could bottle and keep forever.

He dared to brush a lock of hair from her face. Her eyes fluttered closed for a moment, and when they

opened, they were filled with something deeper.... something that mirrored the longing inside him.

"I don't want to wake up," Haruki said, and Aoi only smiled sadly.

When Haruki awoke, he felt the absence of her like a wound.

He couldn't stay in Tokyo anymore.

He had to find her.

Haruki's journey began with naïve hope.

He packed a few clothes, a notebook, and the sketches he had made from their dreams, maps of places

that didn't exist.

He searched for Toshimura across prefectures, getting lost in unfamiliar towns where no one had heard of

it. He slept in train stations and under bus stops, eating convenience store bread, his money leaking away faster than he had planned.

Some nights, overwhelmed by loneliness, he wondered if he was going mad chasing a girl who existed

only in dreams.

But every time he closed his eyes, she was there, waiting by the river, smiling with a sadness he didn't yet

understand.

Weeks passed.

In a crumbling tea shop high in the mountains, Haruki met an old man who listened quietly to his

questions.

"Toshimura... it was real," the man said, voice raspy. "A village lost to time. Burned and abandoned years

ago."

The directions he gave were rough a broken bridge, forgotten paths through tangled forests.

Hope reignited inside Haruki, fragile but burning bright.

The journey was brutal.

The bridge was little more than rotting planks swaying over a roaring river. He crossed trembling, soaked

by rain that made the earth slick and treacherous.

Twice he slipped, bruising ribs and shredding his palms. He had no flashlight, only the stubborn will

inside him.And then — just as despair threatened to consume him, he stumbled into it.

Toshimura.

Silent. Broken. Beautiful in its decay.

Among the ruins, Haruki found a small house still standing.

A woman was kneeling by a patch of wildflowers, her back to him.

Haruki approached cautiously, his heart hammering. "Excuse me... I'm looking for someone. Her name is

Aoi Takamura."

The woman rose slowly. She was older mid-forties perhaps with the same dark hair and gentle features.

"I'm Emiko Takamura," she said carefully. "Aoi was my mother."

Haruki staggered back as if struck.

Before he could think, Emiko asked softly, "How do you know my mother?"

He struggled for words. How could he explain the river, the dreams, the way Aoi's laughter stitched up the

broken places in him?

"I... I met her," he said, voice cracking. "In dreams."

Emiko studied him for a long moment. Not with suspicion, but with something close to sorrow.

Without a word, she gestured for him to follow.

Inside the house, she pulled down an old wooden box. From within, she lifted a photograph — brittle with

age.

It showed Aoi standing under a rain of cherry blossoms, laughing, vibrant, alive.

Haruki reached out, fingers trembling. As he touched the photograph, a jolt ran through him, the memory

of her hand in his, the river's song, her whisper in the wind.

Tears spilled down his cheeks.

Emiko's eyes softened.

"She died of cancer," she said gently. "Twenty years ago. She was only twenty."

Haruki couldn't breathe.

"She passed away... the same day I was born," he whispered, the terrible realization dawning.

Emiko's gaze flickered. Maybe she believed him. Maybe she just saw the grief etched across his face.

Silently, she handed him the photo.

"Come," she said.Through the overgrown paths of the abandoned village, they reached a small graveyard hidden beneath

weeping trees.

In a far corner, a simple stone bore her name.

Aoi Takamura

1980 - 2000

"Forever a dream in bloom."

Haruki fell to his knees before the grave.

The sky wept pink and gold as the sun dipped below the hills.

He laid the photograph carefully against the stone.

Closing his eyes, feeling the cool breeze kiss his face, he whispered:

"Good night, Aoi."

The words dissolved into the wind, carried upward, perhaps into dreams.

CHAPTER II

Aoi's Last Dream

The next morning, Haruki awoke beneath the heavy branches of a weeping tree, feeling the cold breath of

dawn against his skin. He must have fallen asleep by Aoi's grave. His body ached from the hard ground,

but his heart strangely felt lighter, as if some invisible thread had stitched a broken part of him overnight.

He sat up slowly.

Beside him, wrapped carefully in cloth, was a small item Emiko must have left — a folded letter, old and worn.

With shaking fingers, Haruki unfolded it.

The letter was written in delicate handwriting, almost faded now:

"*To whoever finds this,*

If you ever dream of me, please don't cry. Know that even though my time was short, my heart was full. I

will be the river under your stars, the wind in your laughter, the soft step beside your loneliness.

Goodnight, until we meet again.

— Aoi"

Haruki pressed the letter to his chest, closing his eyes.

"Aoi..." he whispered.

Days blurred into each other as Haruki stayed in Toshimura, helping Emiko clean the old house, restoring

what little they could. She treated him like a distant relative who had finally come home. Sometimes, they

shared silent meals; sometimes, they spoke of Aoi.

One evening, as the sun bled gold across the fields, Emiko's daughter a small, curious girl of about seven

tugged at Haruki's sleeve.

"How do you know about Grandma Aoi?" she asked, her big brown eyes blinking.

Haruki knelt, choosing his words carefully. "She found me when I was lost," he said. "She helped me when

I didn't even know I needed help."

The girl tilted her head. "Do you miss her?"

Haruki smiled softly. "Every day."

She took his hand so small in his and said brightly, "I can take you to her special place!"

He followed her as she skipped through wild grasses, up a narrow, hidden path he hadn't noticed before.

At the end of the path stood an ancient cherry blossom tree, gnarled and proud, its branches dancing

even without the wind. Beneath it lay a second grave marker, smaller, older and a circle of river stones.

"This is where Grandma Aoi used to come when she was sad," the girl said, placing a flower at the base.

Haruki knelt again, brushing his fingers along the stones.

The river that had sung to him in dreams... the cherry blossoms... the wild grasses... It was all *her*. Her

memories stitched into this forgotten place.

He sat there for hours, until the stars bled into the sky.

That night, he dreamt again.

Not by the river this time, but under the cherry blossom tree.

Aoi was waiting, just as he remembered.

But something was different.

Her eyes were clearer, her smile softer like someone ready to say goodbye.

She reached for his hand. Their fingers barely touched, but the warmth was there, pulsing gently.

"Thank you for finding me," Aoi said, her voice barely more than a sigh. "Thank you for remembering."

Tears welled in Haruki's eyes.

"I don't want this to end," he choked out.

She smiled sadly. "It's not ending. It's becoming something else."

He didn't understand.

She leaned closer, her forehead resting lightly against his.

"You have a journey too, Haruki," she whispered. "One you must walk awake."

And just like that she was gone.

Haruki woke with the first light of morning, the words still ringing in his ears.

He realized then:

He had spent so long chasing a dream... he had forgotten his own life was still waiting to be lived.

He had to move forward, carrying her memory, not chasing it.

Months Later...

Haruki returned to Tokyo.

But he was not the same man who had left.

He found a small bookstore job, stacking dusty novels and organizing forgotten poetry collections. He

began painting again, something he hadn't touched since his teenage years. His work was different now,

soft rivers, endless stars, black-haired girls smiling under cherry blossoms.Each canvas was a whisper to her.

A promise he had not forgotten.

Sometimes, when the city grew too heavy, he would take the train north, back to Toshimura.

Back to the broken village.

Back to the cherry tree.

He would sit under its shade, reading aloud — old poems, new stories, speaking into the wind, just in

case she was listening.

One evening, as he packed his art supplies after a small local exhibition, a woman approached, a visitor

who had lingered long after others left.

She had kind eyes and carried a notebook filled with messy scribbles.

"I loved your painting," she said, pointing to one canvas in particular, the one of a boy and girl by a river, sending boats into the stars.

"It reminded me," she added shyly, "that sometimes... the people we lose never really leave us."

Haruki smiled.

For the first time in a long while, the smile wasn't painful.

He extended a hand.

"I'm Haruki."

She took it warmly.

"I'm Yuna."

And somewhere, beneath the invisible rivers of the universe.

Aoi smiled too.

Epilogue

The stars still whisper the stories of souls that once crossed paths beyond the realm of time.
Though Aoi's presence faded like a beautiful dream at dawn, her memory remained, lingering in the corners of every heartbeat, in the silent hush of every nightfall.

Some meetings are not meant to last forever — they exist to teach us how infinite a single moment can feel.
And sometimes, in the quiet spaces of life, when the world slows down just enough, we find them again — in a dream, a breeze, a glimmer of moonlight — reminding us that true love never really says goodbye.
It simply transforms... and lives on.

Some loves are like whispers in the wind — soft, fleeting, but eternal in the heart.
— Goodnight Aoi